C

the
Ending

Change the Ending

Stories that matter:
flash fiction about the future
of public life

Curated by Dawn Reeves

sharedpress

First paperback edition published in Great Britain in 2014 by Shared Press

Published by Shared Press
www.sharedpress.co.uk

A catalogue record for this book is available from the British Library.

ISBN 978-0-9574981-3-6

Designed and typeset by Quarto Design
www.quartodesign.com
Edited by Lisa Hughes
www.completefiction.co.uk

Shared Press' policy is to use papers that are natural, renewable and recyclable products from well managed forests in accordance with the rules of the Forest Stewardship Council.

*To everyone who supports and celebrates public service
in tough times, and particularly our writers,
who have sought to change the ending by stretching
their imaginations and courageously
committing their ideas to paper.*

Contents

Foreword

Knowledge Hub is delighted to be involved with *Change the Ending*.

Knowledge Hub is all about challenging and changing the status quo, doing things differently and exchanging aspirational ideas for the future of our public services. We are excited to be part of a creative work like this and it is a pleasure to be able to welcome you to such a stimulating collection of stories about public life.

This volume is a unique contribution to a dialogue that will affect everyone as they go about their daily lives – whether that's as an individual citizen, a member of a community, a user of services or someone who works in or with the public sector. Until now, none of that discussion has been conducted through fiction.

There has been much debate about the nature of public services and local government post-2015/2016. With elections on the horizon, speculation about future budget settlements and too often critical headlines about public service in play, it is vital that we all focus our minds on the future. That is exactly what *Change the Ending* enables us to do.

Knowledge Hub's members are already changing the ending by utilising this free tool to collaborate and innovate, so it's fitting that we are able to support such an inspirational set of stories. Let's make the fiction fact.

Jason Fahy
Executive Director, Knowledge Hub, www.khub.net
October 2014

Introduction

This is a deliberately and deeply unusual book. That's partly because it's a collection of flash fiction – a brief form of literature that challenges writers to tell their tale in anywhere between 300 and 1000 words. This is a deceptive and tricky constraint that tempts writers with little time to think, "That's less than a page – I can do that," and then tests them with the realisation that, while less is often more, less is far from easy. You need to create a character, set a scene, draw your reader into the action and produce a satisfying ending – in this case, in around 350 words.

This is also a collection with a difference because the writers whose work appears here were also challenged by the theme. These are fast and furious stories about a huge and profoundly complex subject – the future of public life, public services and local government. The way we live as individuals and communities, the way we are governed at a local level, which services are provided and how, is complicated. The issues are like a mountain range spanning vast and competing territories with seriously rocky terrain. It's ground rarely covered in fiction.

The premise for the book was that we need to bring fresh, creative thinking to a critical national debate, because too much of that debate is currently in the steely grip of negative narratives. In order to think about what local government is here for and what it should do in the future, my invitation was to step outside the stories of failing bureaucracies, low voter turnout, cuts and decline, and think creatively about the future – a future we want to see.

As someone who's proud to have spent most of my life working in the public sector and who now focuses on facilitating change and creativity, my motivation was to open up a positive, forward-thinking discussion, one that aims to set a different agenda. I wanted to hear what other people thought and felt, to read different stories, to provide a new platform.

I know plenty of creative people who work in local government and public services, and many who don't but who are also interested in and care about it, so although the project regularly felt like a risky undertaking ("You're asking us to do what?") I was confident that stories would emerge.

The submissions published here are genuinely varied and entertaining. What I hoped for were weird, wonderful, wildly imagined tales that confounded stereotypes, gave us glimpses of new futures and made us think. I got all this and more, along with emotion and passion, and warmth and humour.

Some of the stories have a distinctly melancholy feel. There is a sense of wanting to protect what's good about what we have, for the future to be like the past, for the dismantling to end. In the midst of some of the toughest times ever, with potentially worse to come, this isn't surprising. It reflects where we are and that's fair enough; it's what people observe or choose to show. Even in the darkest stories, though, there are glimmers of hope. One child dies, but another is saved. People are pushed to their limits and risk their careers in the hope of change. Doubt and fear appear in the margins, but bravery brings rewards.

Some writers immediately dispensed with boundaries. They imagined future lives, one hurtling forward to a dystopian 2087, others jumping a couple of decades ahead and looking back at lessons learned about what's important. Even where a subject might be predictable, it's been tackled in a unpredictable way – for instance a story about a municipal park imagined from the point of view of the Queen.

There are uplifting stories about people with complex lives, lives that have been changed by the intervention of public sector workers – and vice versa. There are descriptions of small acts that celebrate the often invisible impact of what the sector does and could do more of; that indomitable spirit that holds communities together. The importance of public protection comes through unusual voices – a barge dweller speaks to the importance of paying taxes, a government minister recognises that local government can deal with major disasters.

The collection includes writers taking on knotty political issues with great heart and insight, inviting us to think again about how we care for vulnerable older people, how we make difficult choices about balancing quality and cost, how we value people who work in the public sector, how – and if – we can make the resources stack up.

Changing the ending means changing leadership, changing relationships and changing ourselves. Many stories concern the need for leadership at all levels, of becoming and staying engaged, of holding the ring and doing the right thing in the interests of all our communities. These pieces remind us that we have the skills and capacity to deliver change, that we know what we want and that we will find a way to achieve it.

This has been very much a collaborative project. I have enjoyed working closely with many of the contributors immensely and at the end of the process I am overwhelmed by the quantity and quality of the stories that were submitted. (There are more that we couldn't include in the book on the Shared Press website.) It's left me feeling intrigued about the debate the stories will generate and I feel optimistic. I hope you do, too.

Finally, a big thank you to everyone involved in the project. Thank you so much to Knowledge Hub for supporting the project, and likewise Solace, particularly for encouraging its members to get involved. Thanks, too, to the Guardian Public Leaders Network, which launched the project, and to the production team of editor, Lisa Hughes, and designer, Kate Ferrucci. Most of all, though, thank you so much to all the writers who took the time to share your ideas and work. For many of you this will be the first time you've seen your fiction in print, so thanks for taking up the challenge and being prepared to put yourselves on the line.

Dawn Reeves
October 2014

How It Might Start

He arrives at Clare's house at 11pm and hesitates. It's too late to knock, so he sits in his car, thinking. He's been living in the shadows of Detroit, the spectre of municipal bankruptcy stalking him. He wraps himself in a thin blanket of denial. It couldn't happen here. Surely they wouldn't be the first to go under.

But there's no hiding from it now. Why else would he be here? Hours pass heavily in a flash. His clothes crease and mould.

Clare had offered a solution. "We can put our arms around you." She'd been speaking metaphorically, one council with money to another with none. One chief executive with options to another with… not much time left.

"Come round and have a drink. We can talk, offline," she'd said.

He tries to convince himself that it's the politicians who won't accept the help of a neighbouring authority, but he knows that's only partially true. At this unearthly hour of the morning, there's no escaping himself.

The first light is watery and insubstantial. That's how he feels. He knows be should be pushing back the gloom, putting in support structures, holding up the sky, but he can't do it alone. He has to ask for help, has to admit he's not enough.

He knocks his head against the steering wheel. Come on man, have the conversation!

When a light goes on in the house, his mood improves. Clare answers the door in a soft grey dressing gown that's more like a blanket. In the hallway, the smell of coffee revives him.

"It'll be an investment. We're not interested in a takeover," she says. "And we've got about 30 minutes before I have to get the kids up."

He wonders if they can make it work. What he'll say to the councillors, to the management team, the staff, his wife. It's all a risk.

"We'll make it work," Clare says. "We always find a way."

Back in the car, relief floods his engine. He sits a while longer. It's the right result. The city and their communities need a way forward. The road ahead will be rocky, the navigation a nightmare, but she's given him a new direction.

. . . .

Andy Burns is Director of Finance and Resources at Staffordshire County Council and President of the Society of County Treasurers. This story is the result of a collaboration with Dawn Reeves.

There are People Alive and Trapped in the Town Hall

That's all I need. Another do-gooder.

That's what I thought when I first met Jas, although I didn't say that, of course. He'd knocked on my door one evening; I hadn't been in from work that long.

"Hello, I'm new to the area," he started. "I'm seeing if there's any interest in starting a five-a-side kickabout on the occasional evening, over at the school. Nothing serious, but the first one's tomorrow at eight. Hope I might see you there."

I congratulated him on his initiative, commented on my expanding girth and said I'd try to get along. I had no intention of going.

To give him his due he didn't mention five-a-side again. And I learned later, from Will, that he'd done some sort of deal with the school. Use of the all-weather pitch in return for a few hours' mentoring and coaching from the office types that he rustled up to play.

Another knock on the door from Jas and this time it's some sort of competition to see which part of the town can recycle the most. Actually the kids loved that, ferreting around for every scrap of material. We didn't win, but it was fun.

Another knock on the door… You get the idea.

Ah yes, Will. Before I knew Will was Will, he was the miserable old git that scowled at the kids whenever they rode their bikes up the street. I'd told them to keep away from him. It was only at the street party to commemorate VE Day – you know by now who cajoled us into that – that we all found out that Will was at Normandy.

We also found out that Will loves sport, so now he comes to the pub with a little group of us to watch the mid-week match on Sky. We normally do that after we've had our five-a-side game. Yes, I know!

Jas had one more surprise for me. "Why don't you come along to the council's neighbourhood meeting?" he said. "That's all I need…" I told him.

. . . .

Martin Smith is Chief Executive of the London Borough of Ealing.

Creative Planning

A fresh September morning and two weeks in France had made Diana eager to get back to work. She loved being first into the quiet development control office and settled at her desk, determined to make a dent in the applications backlog. She scanned the files, opening the folder for the former mental hospital site on the city's northern edge.

She'd nearly given up after ten years of the previous appeal-based system, but since the new Planning Act, all publicly owned land and buildings surplus to requirements had to pass through the local planning authority. Her job was to establish the contribution the proposals would make to the local community's future health and wellbeing. Public interest was now firmly at the centre of considerations and although this made the task more complex and challenging, it also brought more innovation and creativity into the process.

Diana was optimistic. Proposals for developing large sites now had to be accompanied by an evaluation of the long-term social returns on investment, an environmental contextualisation assessment and, crucially, evidence of open and transparent consultations with neighbours and local community interests.

Two sets of proposals would be good, to stimulate creative competition from developers and generate local interest. Anticipation building, she clicked on the initial proposals folders and was delighted to find proposals from four local developer consortiums.

All had potential occupiers and included mixed use, sustainable housing, accompanied by, variously, a nursery, school, domestic violence refuge, hospice and further education facility for adults with mental health issues associated with a commercial flower-growing operation which Diana recognised as a successful local business that had outgrown its current site.

Time for a quick cup of tea before making a comparative assessment. She clicked on the revised proposals folder to see if there were any later submissions and was rewarded with two new files. The developers had clearly been talking to each other, the statutory consultees and local community groups. The four original consortiums had skilfully merged into two new teams without compromising the overall integrity of their schemes. Four had gone into two. Could two go into one, she wondered?

. . . .

Pete Murphy is both a planner and a former chief executive of a local authority, with an unquenchable belief in the potential of planning to improve our environments. He lives and works in Nottingham and, despite producing innumerable planning reports, this is his first attempt at fiction.

I Want To Go Now

The carer, slumped in snooze mode in the corner of the room, started at the dying woman's words. Martha had been drifting in and out of consciousness and had not spoken for several hours, but the voice was strong and clear. The carer moved soundlessly through the gloom to the bedside, making a quick visual assessment of the patient. The nurses were not due for several hours.

Although her chest rose and fell with rasping breaths, Martha's eyes were closed and her weathered face remained motionless. The frame of ivory hair fanning across the floral pillow was unusually long and luxuriant for a woman of her age; the carer had delicately combed it for her earlier in the evening, having registered how much it meant to her to look her best. A picture above the bed showed a regal bride with a shy smile, her swarthy, angular husband standing stiffly at her side.

"Martha?" A definite response. "I'm sorry, but before we go on, I need to ask you some questions. Are you saying that you want to end your life?"

As the carer followed the required script, voicing the old lady's repeated affirmations, Martha's daughter leaned in to kiss her mother on the forehead. She softly squeezed the papery hand, forcing down the emotion rising in her core, willing herself to keep it together as the carer confirmed the safe word and gently explained what would happen next.

"I love you, Mum. I'm so proud of you."

The drugs began to drip through the tube.

"She can hear you," said the carer. "She loves you and she wants you to know that she is sure."

A few minutes later, the drugs machine gave a final click.

The carer scanned the bedroom before turning to Martha's daughter.

"Please take as much time as you need. I'll let the relevant people know and they'll be in touch. Can I get you anything?"

Martha's daughter shook her head. "Thank you."

She pressed the button. The carer whirred as it powered down.

. . . .

Sophie Payne fell into public service early and has found it much too interesting and important to leave. A campaigner for 'speaking human', she is inspired by the power of good communications and intrigued by all things digital. Sophie lives and works in Buckinghamshire.

Invasion of the Rubbish Snatchers

 "It was the uniforms," said Derek, trying to read upside-down what the policeman was writing.

"And the flash van," said Cheryl. "It could have been an underground cell. Or the CIA." She pursed her wrinkled lips together tightly. "Rubbish is valuable, Inspector. I've seen a documentary about aliens harvesting our rubbish." Cheryl frowned. "Or maybe it was a film."

Inspector Black continued filling in boxes, without looking up.

"We do need it, you know, to recycle, but once it's gone, it's gone," said Derek.

"Gone?" Inspector Black raised his head.

Derek could see the silent flashing of the last of the ambulances as they left Roseberry Drive, but he looked straight at the policeman. "Yes, gone, to space."

The Inspector turned and gave a thumbs-up to the parked police cars, which obediently started to move, and then to a fire engine, which whooped once and began turning. "The gentlemen were, in fact, just collecting your rubbish." The Inspector closed his notepad. "Outsourced contract. All legit. Whole borough."

"Yes. Sorry."

"I didn't know there'd be a riot van so close by," said Cheryl. "All those guns, Inspector. Very impressive."

"Well, it was ramped up to a code one. The explosives you mentioned."

"Yes." Derek looked down. "You see, I've known our bin men for 15 years, some of them. Where have they gone? The van was so different. I didn't know."

As Derek and Cheryl walked home a week later, the airless hiss of an electric vehicle was suddenly close behind. They held hands tightly. There were footsteps. Derek recognised the blue-grey van as it glided ahead. It was reflective, mirrored even, and advertised Cay Man Resource Relocation.

The broad back of a collector overtook them effortlessly, his heavy boots thumped the pavement and his padded trousers shimmered and creaked. The man turned to give a wide, white-teeth smile, underneath wraparound glasses and a helmet that glinted in the winter sun.

"I knew it," Derek whispered.

"Me too," Cheryl replied.

. . . .

Kate Saffin is a medical doctor and writer.

Lessons in Corporate Parenting

I learnt almost everything I know about being a corporate parent from an extraordinary young woman I met courtesy of Radio 4. She came into my kitchen one Saturday morning, talking straightforwardly about her and her sister's experience of local authority residential care. Her desire to reach out and support other young people whose birth parents were not able to nurture them was palpable.

New to social media, I tweeted about the interview's impact on me. Right back at me came a tweet from Radio 4 connecting me to Kyra. It turned out that she was a recent care leaver and one of 'our children'.

We met in my office just as she was going to uni. We talked a lot about what care leavers really need. Actually, mostly I listened. Sure, we have always had a committed team of 'leaving care' professionals who have navigated fluctuating funding streams and shifting policy approaches. But now we have brought our care leaver children closer to their wider corporate family.

When one young man wanted to be a firefighter, we called the chief fire officer. When someone needed funding to attend an international care leavers' conference, we found it. When a young woman's roof leaked persistently, we didn't get off the phone until it was fixed. We made sure more care leavers got apprenticeships. When we realised just how little the basic apprenticeship left a care leaver to live on, we introduced a 'living wage' apprenticeship.

Uni hoodies, Christmas presents, quick coffees in city centre cafes are all part of our 'corporate parenting' and, yes, on occasion, helping young women, sometimes now with children of their own, to find refuge from abusive partners. We are not perfect parents, but we do want the best for our care leaver children.

And what about our young Radio 4 woman, Kyra? She is now an ambassador for student care leavers and about to have her foundation degree graduation. She cares for various members of her family, older and younger, and is a weekly visitor to her foster mum, who doesn't get out much any more. I am indebted to Kyra.

. . . .

Kersten England is Chief Executive of the City of York Council. Her role is to enable local people and communities to have the best possible quality of life, now and in the future. She is a trustee of Nesta, the national innovation charity, a keen cyclist, hill walker and mother of five young adults.

A New Home for the Bees

"You're acting weird."

Carmen parked the car under a lamp post. The light was fading, time speeding up at the end of the day. "It's alright chickpea. I want to show you something."

The frown on her daughter's face was a rebuke, as fixed as a scar, hardened in the battles of teenage life. "Nah, I'll wait here."

Carmen didn't reply and marched off towards the end of the viaduct. Rosa wouldn't last five minutes alone under the arches, a dormitory of cardboard beds, territory marked by angry graffiti tags.

The path was more overgrown than Carmen remembered. It was a steep scramble up the mound, through brambles and giant buddleias. She heard Rosa stumble, probably on her mobile, but didn't look back.

"Come on love, it won't take long." At the top, Carmen steadied her breath and looked around. The view of the city was stunning. The weeds up here were low, more like a wild meadow. It was too late for the sunset, but the purple light glinted on the disused railway tracks.

"It's going to be a sky-park. It's already an art gallery and an outdoor gym and a natural habitat for…" What had the council ecologist said? A heaven for invertebrates – he'd meant bees, hadn't he?

"It's just your work, isn't it? It's always about you and your work. Why am I even here?"

"Don't you think it's a good idea?"

Rosa began tapping a message on her phone. Carmen buttoned her lip, spotted a couple of breeze blocks and went to sit down. Where was that girl's imagination? Carmen felt inspired. Why didn't her daughter? Young people could help convince the major players to support it. And they would need all the help they could get to make this happen.

Ten minutes passed. Eventually Carmen said, "The bees need you. We need you." Rosa's forehead loosened. "I need you…" Carmen began to doubt her conviction.

The glow of the mobile screen reflected on her daughter's face. "God, Mum. I posted it on Facebook – 143 likes already."

. . . .

Duncan Sharkey is the Managing Director of Worcester City Council. He supports leadership at all levels and has a steadfast commitment to making places better for people to live and work in. This story is the result of a collaboration with Dawn Reeves.

The Fourth Floor

It was a day that whispered a promise of better things. An azure sky lit from the west, cherry blossom drifting on the bare morning breeze. I spotted the van in the distance, two Met officers inside, the sliding door slightly ajar. I wrenched it open with a half-hearted tug. Another officer, disinterested, a cloth sack held securely between his knees.

The journey across the borough quiet but for faint crackles from the radio and a muffled monologue from the driver, the spring brightness now monotone, drifting by with a cinematic reality imposed by the tinted glass.

Pulling into the car park we moved quickly to the communal door. The caretaker, a slight, downcast man in khaki, murmured something and provided access. We filed in, bypassing the dormant lift. The stairwell, pissy and imposing, led upwards.

Four storeys high. There was a brief exchange, a few trivial observations. An official rap at the numbered door, shouts through the letterbox and a final fist-hammer. The officer withdrew the battering ram, gripping his prize like a submachine gun. An explosion. Splitting wood. Fragmenting glass and metal.

The Met officers led, impervious to the festering stench that swallowed us whole. A short passageway, caught on film, the signs everywhere. Blackened bottles. Drug-tainted residue. Everywhere filth and the ominous hum of bluebottles.

Shouting now, the officers moving from room to room. A slight shape sprawled on the bed, an outline seeping onto grey sheets. More flies. An infant at the bars of a cot, stiff and blue. Death-induced vomit from an officer.

It was terrifying. A muffled whimper. Torchlight found a balled up figure beneath the cot. A feral animal. A child. I reached out, breathless as the putrid air invaded me. Coaxing. A touch. Fingers, emaciated and damaged. Too weak to resist. A scramble of arms which clung to me like death itself.

. . . .

Jason O'Brien started life in public services in 1998, with Manchester City Council. He worked in housing for 12 years before qualifying as a social worker and moving to London in 2012. As a working class man from an inner city estate, his professional strength is the personal connection to the families and struggles which he knows first hand.

The Ultimate Challenge

Six. Through and off. Then the bunch, at coffee-shop pace, sounding like a modern-languages class on slick tyres. Team cars stop-start in sympathy with a road missing the selfish jostle of traffic. The voiture balai passes, bringing an unexpected chilly blast, and he is there as I turn away from the road, so close I tread on his brogue.

"Un peu de respecte!", spat out from beneath a dark moustache. Brown eyes, a century older than the rest of him, flash challenge. "But, mes p'tits gars chéris du Yorkshire, you think it is you who are les patrons aujourd'hui, non?"

I know him, of course. "Monsieur Desgrange?" He responds with a comically over-done Gallic shrug, stubbing a spent Gauloise under his scuffed toes. I catch myself bowing slightly. "Not at all, sir. This is your race. Your creation. Your genius. Your gift."

One side – the left – of his moustache twitches. A smile maybe, or a snarl. "Sacrebleu," he grunts, then, heavily accented, "listen very carefully…"

"I hid for much of that first Tour de France, in 1903…" Another Gauloise has appeared, magically aglow and spreading its pall like incense in an airy cathedral. He clearly wants to talk. I listen, very carefully. "Not even my idea, you know. That idiot Lefèvre's. No cycling man. A desperate measure to put one over on those 'salauds' at *Le Vélo*. Of course, it went well. I emerged to take the credit."

Henri, smokily indistinct, pauses – ethereal. I speak. "But you believed in human endeavour, surely? In heroism and resilience? In achieving the unthinkable? In the health and identity of a People? Hell, man, you were a rider yourself! You invented le Tour because you believed these things."

Perhaps it is the Gauloise, but Desgrange's eyes are misty. "Non. Mais non. I saw le Tour grow and only then I believed. A bicycle race to sell my paper; it became le Grand Boucle, speaking for my nation and my sport. A bicycle race to sell your Yorkshire… ça va!" Again the elaborate shrug. "Now let it speak for you. What will you have it say?"

. . . .

With a background in arts marketing, **John McPherson** started in local government promoting the cultural sector. Over the years he developed an interest in staff engagement and how people deal with change; these are his main areas of work at Leeds City Council. Outside work he is prone to serial obsessions.

Enough

She was exhausted, she told the doctor, her friends, her colleagues and her family. The advice included: take time off sick, sleep more, take anti-depressants and – from everybody – look after yourself.

One Thursday in February, she stared at her Year 11 French class. Some of them were struggling to stay awake. The others were restive and challenging. Anne had no idea how most of them were going to achieve their target grades. *Her* target grades. She didn't have it in her to coax and bully every last one to the finish line this time.

Anne resolved to take the universal advice. She went home at 5pm, leaving work behind. She ate slowly and well. She went to bed early. The next day, she rose later than usual and arrived at school at 8am. Her colleagues looked at her warily. Had she lost it? They'd seen it before. It frightened everyone.

Anne worked hard until the lunch bell went. She drove to the park. After walking for precisely 20 minutes, she ordered minestrone soup in the café. She read her book. She was back at school five minutes before afternoon classes began.

She continued this pattern day in, day out. She spent time with friends and took long bike rides at the weekend. She resisted pressure to stay up late or check emails or complete household chores. Things went undone. Homework wasn't marked and laundry wasn't up to date. She ignored it.

By results day in August, her energy was high and expectations were low. In the face of severe criticism, she hadn't run after-school classes or lunch-time revision sessions. Everyone, including herself, expected her to leave teaching soon.

But she had also noticed that her to-do list was shorter, only consisting of things that *really* had to be done. She found she was faster, more decisive. Over the months, her surprised students no longer expected her to spoon-feed them. Her family had begun to tackle domestic tasks that they hadn't even realised existed before she stopped doing them.

Her class didn't meet their targets. They exceeded them.

. . . .

Sarah Dale is an occupational psychologist and coach who works with a range of individuals and organisations, including those in local government, higher education and professional services. She is the author of two non-fiction books – *Keeping Your Spirits Up* and *Bolder and Wiser*, both of which reflect mid-life and mid-career themes that she often encounters in clients (and in herself and friends!)

I Walk the Line

Bodies crash to the ground, mud flies, legs whirl. Finally a ball fires out of the mess of players, hits the bar and bounces down. At the other end the goalie dances a celebratory jig, while his teammates round on the ref. "Goal! It crossed the line!" All eyes turn to the man in black...

All except Bill's. His gaze is fixed on the chalky white line that separates elation and disappointment. The line he'd carefully marked out that morning, and every Saturday morning since before those lads were even born.

Some of them thought that was his only job – marking out the lines. They were in double maths when he was mowing, cutting back the hedge, picking up dog muck or clearing out the shinpads and underpants they left behind every week. In a way, though, they were right. Marking the lines had always been the icing on the cake; a neat finish to the week.

The ref stands still, replaying the incident in his head. Bill still stares at the line. It was, as he'd proudly told his mates in the pub the night before, "the end of the line" for him – 39 years, 640 yards, six pots of chalky paint, every week.

Some of the kids he'd seen play had grandchildren out there now. Of course, they'd never been any good. Down the years a couple had had trials for local clubs. One had become a chess grandmaster though! But this lot, finally, had something. Hang on to a draw here and they'd win the league.

The council had given him a good send off – nice sandwiches and a lovely speech – but he couldn't wait to get back to his pitch. He'd checked every blade of grass for this one and pushed his line machine with steady purpose.

The ref lifts his head, demanding respect. "No goal," he announces. "I saw it clearly. Never crossed the line."

"Of course it bloody didn't – not my line, not today," mutters Bill, as he treads down a divot.

. . . .

Adrian Besley writes sports and humour books, and believes the public sector should be defended. He lives in North London.

Instagram Sam

Here he comes, look: old as the river itself, sliding out of the lock, two barges strapped together to save fuel. Instagram Sam, we call him, because if you're not acquainted you'd say there's no way he really looks like that. Not in the 21st century. Skipper's cap and his neck wrapped round with a red scarf like a Wurzel. His green eyes bright in his coal-dust face. Hand-chalked board propped on the fore deck, telling you what he'll do a sack of coal for, a litre of red diesel.

He spots me holding the boy, salutes with his tea-hand, drains the mug because he knows he's getting a top up. Strong, milky, two sugars: I've made it a hundred times. Part of the fee. Used to be he'd take our bins as a freebie if we bought his coal, but he's got the contract now, proper wages, our cash since they agreed to take Council Tax from us.

Sam says we're idiots piping up when we were getting away with it, but that's what people don't see. You're not getting away with anything when you're evicted every sodding year, even with your kids, even with the perfect stretch of towpath you've strimmed and pruned and made into a garden. Yeah, the bins are good, but knowing you're legit, that no one's boarding you at 5am like a band of hi-vis pirates: that's the big change.

"Still here then, my lover," he calls out, whacking the old Lister into reverse to slow, then cutting it.

"Still here."

I put my boy down on the deck and he toddles off, lobbing his half-chewed gingerbread man at a duck, hitting her square on the beak. We laugh. Sam tosses the old tin mug over and I catch it and, Jesus, it's worse than usual. I dangle the thing between my finger and thumb and say, "Christ alive, Sam, you've got a bloody sink," and he shrugs and swings the tiller and he's alongside us. He chucks us a line, ties up, hops on. The kettle sings from the cabin.

. . . .

Kate Simants is a writer and mother from Bristol, where she lives with her family on a barge on the Avon. She is a founding member of a moorings cooperative and has lived afloat most of her adult life. Kate is currently working on her second novel.

Who Are Yer?

He stuffs his City scarf into his sports jacket. "I don't follow. Identity? What about it? There's nothing wrong with my identity."

"You mean, I'm all right Jack?" Anita replies.

His fellow councillor can be pretty abstract. His mind wanders. That's a 1950s comedy. "Well, yeah. I am." He can see she looks irritated.

"But not everyone's sure of their identity, are they? Les, you need to go and talk to those lads – the ones hanging out on the steps of the town hall."

"Security'll deal with them."

"It's our job to help them secure a new identity."

"Is it?"

"It is! We need to help them build a sense of solidarity with their communities."

"We need to build housing!" He's quite pleased with that.

"We don't want them to get trapped into an oppositional narrative."

"Never did me any harm."

"No, because you were able to secure your interests through established identities – your estate, your football club, your union, your party. What've these kids got? Private rented, an X-box habit, gangs and Russell bloody Brand." She draws her eyebrows up and back like a crossbow. "So they're just hoodies or looters? That's who you think they are?"

"I didn't say that."

"It's an opportunity for us to do something positive. Go and talk to them. Ask how we can empower them to assert their own interests."

. . . .

"Another pint, mate?"

"So I said I'd talk to them. No one's told them how their school got built, why there's a dispersal order at the bus station, who does what, who owns what. It's informed civic engagement." He wants them to know he's not the enemy. He wants to know who they want to be. And maybe the council can help them make something of themselves. He hopes they turn up. If not he'll find out where they live. In a good way.

"You feeling alright, Les? Shall I get these."

. . . .

A consultant and facilitator supporting creative change in public services, **Dawn Reeves** is currently working on the follow-up to her town hall thriller, *Hard Change*. Find out more at www.dawnreeves.com. She is a former local authority corporate director. Change the Ending was her idea and she's made it happen.

Rumble-strip

The sudden juddering of the rumble-strip jolted me from momentary sleep. Concrete pillars in my headlights, then the whole bloody lot flashed before me – just like they always say.

A blue ball in long grass. New T-bar sandals. A gritty picnic on a wind-burned beach. Sums on squared paper: hundreds; tens; units. My first wristwatch. Coming third in the running race. Carol concerts' itchy wings and halos. The dog's dead. Mum crying. Snowball fight. A funeral.

Flashing by: secondary school; university; first job; white wedding. More funerals. More tears. Second job. Second marriage. New start.

Bathing an old man. He has sore legs. Dab him dry, gently. Pouring trolley-loads of suppertime drinks, milky and sweet, straight from the spout.

A fight. Handwriting notes in triplicate. Manilla folders tightly packed in metal cabinets. Lost the key. Can't leave without locking up. Panicking. Flushed.

On a visit: house stinks of cat crap. She's dead. The neighbours called. We didn't know her. It's the constable's first one. He spews up on the doorstep. It's a mess.

New job, computer, team. All at sea.

A sing-a-long: an ancient, bony hand claws softly at my elbow; a trembling jaw carefully, quietly enunciates, "It's good here."

Years flash by. Council empires rise and fall. Cuts and mergers bring out the placards. I travel across counties to keep in work.

There's no bingo now. No council homes. Our folk sit alone, Skype from time to time and order grub online.

Colleagues, like seasons, flutter in and out of frame. I age in the mirror. I glimpse myself in shop fronts – suited, greyer than before. My handbag holds a magical, glossy pane through which I view every report, budget or email and every care record of every individual in our protective embrace.

I'm late for an evening meeting 70 miles away. My car blinks its welcome. I sling my bag on the passenger seat. A satisfying clunk of the door. I'm in. I check the rear view mirror and pull away.

Last thing: the sound of my slate cracking the windscreen; the pillars and the rumble-strip.

. . . .

Pippa Corner has been working in health and social care for 20 years, in the NHS and local authorities, as well as a short spell at the Audit Commission. She has held several senior roles with a focus on partnership and integration, and is currently a head of service at Calderdale Council.

Triple H

"So, what's it to be today?" s/he thought. "Heaven or Hell?"

Every day is like a game of chance: nothing guaranteed, just www. thefates.gov.uk deciding whether or not to mess with your head. And your arms, legs and just about everything else – especially on a bad day.

But, of late, there was a third "H". Hope. Distant, often out of reach, but, nonetheless, forming inexorably and coming closer.

When younger (yesterday, an age ago – both were true), s/he reflected, two things could be relied upon. First, others found it easier to cope with you because you were small and you were still sweet and the differences didn't show so much, so it didn't seem to matter as much. Secondly, nobody expected very much from you, very much of you. All shocking. All shockingly un-shocking. Normal really. Ha!

But now there were signs of change. As if under the influence of a stubbornly recurrent perigee moon, the tide was turning – and staying turned. White crests were forming. Waters were beginning to boil. Waves might just come crashing sometime soon onto the shores of complacency.

Valuing difference might just become the new normal. People might ask you, not ask about you. People might expect of you, not of others. It looked like they might actually even care – care about you, but not for you. You want the chance to do that for yourself. Yes, with encouragement, with support, with challenge (and with setbacks – just like everyone else), but without that crushing passivity that was so well meaning, but so disempowering.

Like the great man said, "Don't stop; give it all you got." And I've got Hope. Just like you. I hope.

. . . .

Mark Rogers is Chief Executive of Birmingham City Council and President of Solace.

The Wedding

Nobody could say theirs was a conventional love affair, particularly Grandpa, an ex-Mayor and sage about all things councils would do.

Amy and Holly met not in the bar or workplace and, though they met online, it wasn't a dating group either. Both, from opposite ends of the borough and social strata, were volunteer flood wardens. In the 2013 floods, volunteer wardens posted readings online about rising water levels in communities which directed the council's response to the changing situation. Both shared a similar wit and were keen users of the Facebook page the council had set up.

It wasn't long before online conversation became a face-to-face meeting and from there love had grown. Grandpa was perfectly understanding about his granddaughter Amy marrying another woman, but he couldn't get his head around the volunteer warden stuff: "What, no bridge engineers on call out taking readings?!"

Amy and Holly's business came from those early social media forays, as they developed a local solution to loneliness, connecting older people to local services, and volunteers to befriend them via social media. Grandpa found all that new-fangled, too, and said that in his time at the council there was no choice stuff, with money used to get the services folk wanted. In his day, it was get what you were given.

This last year was change all round. Holly had led on getting their new home, well, new to them. It was one of the derelicts by the railway they said nobody would live in, blighting the local community. The council said millions were needed to demolish and rebuild. Then an energetic councillor and local people said, "Let's give them away and ask people to do them up." That's what they had done, making them energy self-sufficient with solar panels made by residents.

So there was money for today's wedding in the old council chamber, restored by the trust that owned it with lottery funds, and affordable because catering and flowers were being done by college students learning a trade. The council had definitely changed since Grandpa's day!

. . . .

Jo Miller is Chief Executive of Doncaster Metropolitan Borough Council.

Emergency

The fluorescent lights of the Cabinet Office briefing room threw the Minister's dilemma into stark relief: responsible for the unfolding emergency on the one hand, but chained to a Whitehall desk on the other.

The last 48 hours had tested her every nerve, and the combination of sleepless nights and coffee-fuelled days was taking its toll. Around the briefing room table, the enquiry into the cause of the catastrophe and the need to deal with its aftermath merged into a confusing mêlée of words; urgent yet curiously abstract, because there was no hard evidence or much accurate information to inform them.

The Minister craved a walk in the fresh air. The second day after the disaster was drawing to a close and it would be dark in Downing Street, but that wouldn't stop the media frenzy which would ensue if she were to step outside.

The civil servants and military officers were doing their best, of course, but with communication systems compromised, even getting an accurate picture from the scene was extremely difficult. Nor were the Prime Minister's interventions helping. He was on his way home from holiday, having initially underestimated the scale of events, and was now compensating by issuing Churchillian demands for "action this day" with no intimations about exactly what the action should be.

However, the hourly situation reports – or 'sit reps' as the naval officer in charge of the briefing room insisted on calling them, to the Minister's intense irritation – were gradually becoming clearer.

Things were still bad, but not perhaps as bad as the first day's traumatic scenes of a break-down in civil order had suggested.

Indeed, it appeared that the immediate response to the emergency had actually been more effective than was first evident in Whitehall. What had looked like large numbers of stunned and disorientated refugees was, in fact, a well-organised evacuation of the disaster area by the local council, clearing the way for the emergency services to tackle the deluge.

As she pushed back her chair, the Minister's last thought before falling into involuntary sleep was, "Thank God for the local authority."

. . . .

Jan Britton is Chief Executive at Sandwell Council in the West Midlands and was previously Sandwell's director for urban regeneration. Jan is proud to be a career local government officer and has also worked at Buckinghamshire, Colchester and the London Borough of Barking and Dagenham. Jan has a wife and four children who tolerate his obsessive commitment to work and old cars.

Chicken Chow Mein for the Soul

It had been a big day for Stephanie; the sort of day that deserved a celebratory beer and a Chinese takeaway; the sort of day that came very rarely for a hard-working but underappreciated social care commissioner. After eight months she was about to deliver a new home care contract for the council.

Whereas previously some areas of the borough had had spotty coverage, there would now be multiple providers in every area and, most importantly, Stephanie had saved the council an incredible £3 for each hour of care delivered. It was no wonder she had been roundly congratulated, so why didn't it feel quite right?

Just five years out of university, Stephanie was committed, intelligent and ambitious. Admittedly it was a sign of the times that someone so young had been asked to lead this crucial piece of work, but she had done well and a promotion was on the cards, so why hadn't she ordered her chicken chow mein yet?

At the back of her mind she knew why. Although the contract was a great deal for the council and therefore the local tax payer, the companies providing the care would need to find a way to absorb those cost-savings and that meant paying their staff even less.

They had to cover administration charges, management overheads, travel costs, holiday pay, sick pay, pension contributions and a small amount of profit out of that hourly payment, which left very little for the people actually delivering the care. This nagged away at the young local government worker; the people looking after people like her sick grandma were now going to be paid a lot less.

Had she struck the right balance? She wasn't sure, but she did know she hadn't had a choice and she'd enabled the council to deliver the most significant savings in the history of local government without taking services from the vulnerable people they served.

It was a big day and Stephanie ordered her chow mein and had her beer. She'd done a good job and deserved it. It just didn't quite taste as sweet as she had hoped.

. . . .

Gareth Young is a local government officer and the co-author and presenter of the popular welovelocalgovernment blog and podcast. Follow him on twitter @gyoun82

Democracy Maintained...

David sat in the full council meeting. He gave a cursory nod to George, the council's solicitor, and Jan, the chief executive, and went back to reviewing the paper that would recommend members made the biggest political decision of their lives; a decision that would change local government for ever; a political earthquake that would affect a generation. To oversee the takeover – wasn't that why he was here? Even Whitehall was looking in.

Middletown DC was a relatively small district council in sleepy East Anglia. David's predecessors had struggled for years to balance the books and members had pressed for ever more vicious externalisation of services – 'strip out this, strip out that – it's all waste' had been the mantra. Now the chickens had come home to roost. Costs were spiralling, but the finance team itself had been cut to the bone, left powerless against the outsourcing behemoths, and the council was facing bankruptcy.

Members were clearly complicit in the imminent acquisition. They had insisted on signing the contracts. They had disregarded the crippling terms and conditions. David knew the smell of conspiracy was like a rotting banana skin – and this one had been rotting for years.

David had been parachuted in three weeks ago to replace the outgoing chief financial officer. 'Outgoing'? Poor fella. Shafted more like. He'd given 30 years' loyal service to these members, but continual underinvestment had meant he hadn't been able to keep pace. His departure had removed the final obstacle and only two days later a fully costed and legaleased merger report had been circulated. It had clearly been prepared by the county, which was funny, really, given that three-quarters of the Middletown members were also county members.

David, George and Jan stood up. David boomed for attention and started the PowerPoint. There, in full technicolour, was a picture of the leader counting cash with the director of the refuse contractor. The room was stunned into silence. David didn't need to look at George and Jan, he could feel their relief. All three knew democracy had been maintained. Even Whitehall might be pleased. On cue, the police walked in!

. . . .

A district council chief finance officer and member of the Chartered Institute of Public Finance and Accountancy (CIPFA), **Clive Mason** has worked in local government for 27 years, mostly within either accountancy or internal audit. Unusually, he has also worked for a private sector consultancy, helping councils through tough financial times.

Demmed

Avonmouth.city 2087.

David raised himself from his pillow, a sweaty sheet swathed around him. His desres was making tiny animal sounds of concern. There was a faint knocking at the front door. Nobody knocked at a front door. The desres raised the lights softly as he got up into the darkness of what he now saw was 5am, written in green script on the wall.

"Shut up," he said. Its mewling ceased. The knocks were now accompanied by a muffled voice.

"A little boy's told me! The little boy!" The projection showed a flabby man of early middle age in a maroon dressing gown patterned with grey diamonds.

"Hello?" David said through the audio. "You've got the wrong place. If you're locked out, call the Network. It will sort you out."

The man knocked harder. "Chateau d'Oix," he said, smiling now. "I'm going skiing in Chateau d'Oix!"

Where the piste would have melted many years ago. The visitor might not have been as helpless as he seemed. An ID cop had plenty of enemies. The man's hands were shoved into his dressing gown. What did he have in there?

David opened the door. He needed to see him in the flesh, felt a basic urge to go offline – as though to step into the open air could achieve that. The air was tepid. Avonmouth.city hummed. Wind turbines span slowly in the near-above.

The desres' mewling became a loud whistle of alarm. David overrode it with a gesture. The man put on a sickly smile. "Bastard!" he said. "Shitting bastard!"

There was no mistaking it now. He really was a dem. Escaped from a carie. David's own life in the Network flashed before him. Two flesh in dressing gowns facing one another, bleary.

"Wait here," David said and turned to go inside.

"David."

"What did you say?" David swung back. The cold seeped deeper into his feet, numbing the bones.

"David a good boy." The man looked down at David's hand gripping his arm. "Bastard. Good bastard. Voodooed."

. . . .

Tim Kindberg (champignon.net) is a creative technologist based in Bristol and the man behind Nth Screen. He has had poems and short stories published, and is the author of the crossover fantasy novel *Shadows of Marrakech*. This story is an edited extract from *Take You With Me*, a novel in progress.

Caped Crusader

So I'm going along through the forest – usual route; same trees, grass, rocks.

Having become emboldened due to the fact I forgot my sandwiches, I'm heading off-piste.

Sometimes you gotta take risks and, yes, it can be scary, but the end results can be surprising.

Now don't get me wrong – I'm not daft. I haven't met this wolf character (big eyes and teeth apparently) and things could get ugly. But honestly, what are the options? Take the chance that we won't be wolfed down for dinner?

I reckon that if enough of us forge new paths through the forest we can shave some serious time off the journey. Not only that – more routes = more options = less being eaten.

It's like this girl in my class – Rapunzel (home-schooled for a while). She got fed up and said, "Tell you what. Let's cut the hair, weave it into a big fat rope and then I can get out. Anyone who wants to climb up can knock themselves out."

My family are, er, *financially constrained* and it can be hard seeing all the shiny new toys and not touching. The spoilt brat next door (Goldilocks – only child) with all the Barbies, she never fully appreciates them; will never know the absolute joy of finding a bargain or a freebie. We, however, make 'horses' out of dogs and castles on the stairs.

The Hood motto? Think really creatively and not outside the box for goodness sake. Use the darn box. Use the tape, staples, labels and tear it apart to make sure every single scrap of it finds purpose.

We do stuff better than anyone because we have to. *Need* is king, queen and knave in our house. It's like shopaholics anonymous (except not, er, anonymous). Yes, I want it, but do I really need it? If I really *do* need it, what's the best value for money for everyone in our extended family? Can others use it too and can it grow with us? Like hand-me-down capes. I know a lot about those...

. . . .

Rebecca Smith is, in her own words, incredible and, she says, probably a genius. Working in the communications team at Buckinghamshire County Council she is given fantastic opportunities to do a gazillion different things. Her finest hour was using her shoe to get a cabinet member into a locked office. Don't even ask...

Catherine to the Rescue

I felt I was drowning... in both booze and forms.

Both my partner and I had just turned 24, but our lives felt over already. Two screaming kids under five, squeezed into my mother-in-law's small terraced house with barely a penny to our name.

Out of the blue I got a call from Catherine at the council. She explained she had been going through my customer account. I didn't even know I had one or what it was.

Middle-aged, Catherine knew a thing or two about life and took no prisoners. She was somehow different from the rest. Pushy, but empathetic; nothing I said to her seemed to faze her.

She seemed to know a lot about me, including that we had money problems and had been kicked off the housing register, because I was out of work. She spent time with me exploring what I was good at; that was a novel experience. I had always fancied myself as a bit of a cook – it was my homemade lasagne that had hooked Joyce, my partner, in the first place – but had no idea how to get myself properly trained or to present myself to a prospective employer.

Catherine got me into a work club at the library. It was good to go somewhere which felt neutral and free from the stigma that oozes from the very fabric of the job centre.

The club helped me put together a CV, set up an email account and search the web for opportunities. They encouraged me to approach a company that the council had persuaded to come to the area to develop a new leisure complex. I was given a trial with one of the restaurants in the complex. Because I turned up on time and did my best, they took me on as a trainee chef.

It's still tough. But I feel better about myself; we seem to be getting our life under control. If I can make a go of the job, we may be able to get a home of our own. That prospect gives me something to hold on to.

. . . .

Twenty years as a local authority chief executive in four different authorities has done nothing to dent **Richard Carr**'s eternal optimism about the positive impact councils can have on people's lives. His story is entirely fictitious but draws on examples of some of the practical ways many councils are supporting struggling residents to get their lives back on track.

Left Behind

As he stepped in front of the approaching train, the images flashing past Donald's eyes were almost exclusively work-related. This was no surprise to Donald, given that he had spent the majority of his waking hours at work, for the council, an organisation he had joined on leaving school, 22 years ago.

Donald was not surprised, on launching himself from the platform, that the first scene to enter his mind was of his open-mouthed colleagues, earlier that morning, arriving back from their walking meeting to find him sprawled on the floor of their newly refurbished, open-plan office, carefully cutting out an assortment of letters from various newspapers, both capital and lower case, and sticking them onto some paper. What was the world coming to when a man couldn't write a resignation letter in private anymore? Everywhere a bloody audience.

Neither was Donald surprised, landing feet first on the train tracks, to visualise his manager, Cynthia, in the contemplation pod that lunchtime, embarking on her daily meditation session, eyes closed, palms together, headphones on, oblivious to Donald's pounding on the glass walls of this fishbowl, blind to the carefully constructed resignation letter that he was holding up to the window. Ah, Cynthia. A daily presence in his life. Always telling him to take a break, book some leave, look after himself.

They were all like her these days. Always worried about *wellbeing at work*. It was as if they simply didn't accept the need to set an example to your staff by working hard and working long hours, didn't understand that looking up from your job does no good and that 12-hour days never did him any harm.

What did come as a surprise to Donald was that he appeared to be still alive, still clasping his letter. As the train whooshed past him on the opposite platform, he listened to the silence, feeling the eyes of many looking down on him on his lowly stage. Suddenly, he felt a strange sense of wellbeing. He put his palms together, closed his eyes, and started to hum.

. . . .

Jenny Hacker works as a consultant in public health in Croydon, where she leads on workplace health, health intelligence, knowledge management and training. She started her local government career in housing, before training as a researcher and public health specialist. She is a keen writer, tennis player and Arsenal fan.

Park Life

It did seem familiar, now, the town, as the train slowed to a crawl outside the station. Decades ago she'd come by the same route and she suddenly remembered how it had looked then: new homes for new families springing up along the railway line, homes fit for heroes back from the war; the schools, libraries, community centres for citizens to enjoy, designed, built and looked after by people in the town hall, recreating neighbourhoods for their people from slums and bomb-ravaged streets.

Today, though, even in the crisp sunshine of an early summer's morning, the place looked faded and tired. She sighed. So much had changed since those early, hopeful years. But the park was as she remembered it. Of course, she had seen hundreds like it over the years, but there was something about this one that had stayed in her memory: the flowerbeds of cheerful red, yellow and white flowers in careful rows, occasionally breaking out into a swirling circle of colour; the bandstand, sparkling and freshly painted; and, above all, the grass. Emerald green, beautifully striped and welcoming for families spreading a picnic rug, Tupperware and toys for an afternoon in the sun, teenagers gathering to giggle and share secrets, and young lovers stretched out, side by close side.

Accustomed to her own acres of private park, her hundreds of miles of tended lawns, it suddenly struck her that parks like this were the green jewels in the crown of every town and city. Mostly people took for granted the years of tender care that had gone into them, the skills of the gardeners nurturing the young bedding plants every spring, the patient clearing-up after busy, messy bank holiday weekends. Parks built by her people, owned by her people and lovingly preserved for future generations.

Today her return, half a century since her first visit, would remind the town, for a morning, at least, that their council still did some things pretty well, and the thousands who cheered her slow parade along the well-tended paths agreed that the park had never looked better, the council had done a splendid job in making it look beautiful, and that the town had done Her Majesty proud.

. . . .

Fran Collingham is an assistant director at Coventry City Council where she's in charge of the communications team. She began her career as a journalist before joining local government as a press officer nearly 20 years ago.

My Arranged Marriage

I thought I'd avoided it, but here I am stuck in an arranged marriage. In my case, my parents are Public Health England and my in-laws are NHS England. I haven't suffered domestic abuse or anything like that, but I do feel I'm always expected to wash up in both houses, to show my gratitude for being rescued from 'being on the shelf'.

Am I happy in my marriage? Actually, I am. I bounce out of bed with a spring in my step every morning. My partner is great. He makes me laugh, encourages me and wants me to be emotionally fulfilled, but I'm not convinced my in-laws feel the same.

You're living dangerously. That's what my friend and colleague said when I told her I'd signed an open letter voicing strong objections to the latest dictats. Was she right? Could someone in my position be politically active without being exchanged for a more compliant model or simply getting the chop?

It nearly happened a year ago. I got a visit from the in-laws saying my paper work wasn't in order and they would be forced to terminate my marriage. The fact that they had lost the contract was apparently irrelevant. I had to apply to get married again.

And yesterday we were called to the in-laws' house to hear the news that more divorces are going to be necessary. This is particularly galling given the proposals, which, in the unlikely event of us being successful in finding a new partner quickly, will allow the patriarch to retain an ongoing financial interest in former daughters-in-law.

My in-laws' extended family is the largest in Europe. Why would it want to cut people like me off? It's so short-sighted given the significant contribution we make to our overall health and wealth.

Of course I know any relationship takes effort, but I am resolved that while I have breath in my body I will keep fighting the injustices, I will continue to live dangerously, because I don't have any other option and because, although the in-laws may not always believe me, I really am committed to making my marriage work.

. . . .

Thara Raj is a locum consultant in public health at Public Health England. Joining the NHS in 1987 after publication of the Ottawa Charter and Black Report, she fights health injustices using evidence as her weapon. Thara enjoys performing, including football, stand-up comedy and as a pandemonium drummer.

The Only Source of Knowledge is Experience

Sandy had thought that after 30 years as a clerk nothing work-related could surprise him, but when he realised that the planning decision on the website had been altered from rejection to approval he had been momentarily stunned.

The proposed new housing estate had been rightly condemned for making no provision for either community facilities or affordable housing and now the management team were in despair, because they *knew* that the only other record was the developer's video, which had been deviously edited to make it appear that the application had been agreed. The councillors would be furious and heads would roll.

"Whose job is it to ensure that the council's decision-making records are properly kept?" the rotund man on Sandy's left thundered.

Well, thought Sandy that would be yours as director of ICT, but in these circumstances the blame usually falls on the most junior officer in the room, which of course would be...

"Sandy! How could the records that your section keeps have been altered!?"

"Through the chairman," Sandy countered, while studiously ignoring the incandescent director to his left, "I refer the meeting to Local Government Act 1972, Schedule 12 Paragraph 41(1)." None of them knew the reference, but none of them would admit this, nor had they openly challenged Sandy's decision to hold the meeting in the library.

Sandy retrieved an impressive leather-bound book from the shelf above the bewildered director's head and, pausing only to find a pre-marked place, presented it with an understated nod to the chief executive. "The Act states that all minutes of the meeting are signed as a correct record." All eyes turned to the paper copy of the decision, which faithfully recorded the rejection of the planning application.

As despair now transformed into boisterous delight, only one officer maintained his professional composure – second nature to an experienced clerk. Sandy wistfully pondered how long it would be before paper records were consigned to the recycling bin of history. Well, he concluded, at least I'll be retired by then.

. . . .

Patrick Adams has worked as a democratic services officer at South Cambridgeshire District Council for the last 13 years, although for much of that time he enjoyed the more self-explanatory title of 'committee clerk'. His favourite saying is, 'It doesn't matter who you vote for, the Government always gets in.'

A Rainy Day

That sickening ping of an email. "Simon, see me in my office at 11am." Short and sweet – or short and sour more like.

Simon had been museums manager at the council for seven years. He'd arrived with a suitcase full of ideas, determined to revitalise the service, but once immersed in the role had found a group of dedicated, knowledgeable people. They spent their days talking to visitors, enthused excited children with grizzly stories, spoke at care homes about the impact of the First World War. He'd realised that the passion and commitment to bring heritage to life was already there.

Hanging on for survival was a state of mind for his team. They were used to cuts and operating in a creaky building, even when the council had money to spend, but the whiff of anxiety was now all-consuming as everyone wondered when the final act would be announced. Simon walked into his boss' office as the town hall clock chimed eleven. What came next took him a while to process.

"Thanks for coming in at short notice, Simon. I've been contacted by the managing director of the company doing the museum repairs. They've found a document beneath the floorboards. It contains information about a fund no one knew about. It states that £5 million has been left to redevelop the site by an American who visited when on holiday in the 1980s. He only went in to escape the rain, but the kindness shown by the staff clearly made a big impression."

Simon's head was spinning. He had heard rumours that the closure of the building was inevitable. He had walked into the room ready to face the music, but walked out holding a tatty, dusty document with a newly broken seal that he gripped tighter than anything he had ever held before.

One act of kindness on a rainy day over 30 years ago and Simon could rewrite the story for future generations of his town. He stumbled out of the town hall into the sunshine with a new script already forming.

. . . .

Robin Tuddenham is Director of Communities and Business Change at Calderdale Council.

Upwardly Mobile

Every other Tuesday, halfway through my shift in the village shop, I'd watch the white mobile library bus trundle past on its way to park by the village school. On its return trip 20 minutes later, the lady driver would wave cheerfully to me. In our narrow lane, the giant books painted on the side of the van almost touched the shop window, making me feel the size of a Borrower, which was ironic, because I'd never borrowed any of its books.

Then, at the start of October, my hours at the shop were cut. Our takings had been falling since the new superstore popped up a few miles away. After that, I was always at home on Tuesdays, alone in my cottage opposite the school. I'd watch the library van park outside my house.

As soon as its doors swung open, school children bearing books would bound up its steps. Older folk followed more slowly, cautiously gripping the handrail with their book-free hand. When they emerged, one by one, they'd all be smiling, large print books a common bond between the very old and very young.

As the days shortened, I grew weary of daytime television. I wished I could afford more bus trips into town or to anywhere that would make my life less dull. Then last Tuesday afternoon I finally found my courage. Once its regular visitors had dispersed, I slowly mounted the mobile library's steps.

"Can I help you, dear?" asked the lady driver, now standing behind the counter. It seemed odd to hear her voice at last.

"I don't know," I faltered. "You see, I'm not much of a reader."

When she ducked behind the counter, I thought it was to hide her scorn, but she popped up again with a library card application form and a pen.

"Ooh, everyone's a reader, dear!" she exclaimed kindly. "You just haven't found the right books yet. We've got something here for everyone. I'll help you choose."

But that's all I have time to tell you now, because I want to get back to my book.

. . . .

Debbie Young is an author (her latest book is the flash fiction collection *Quick Change*), journalist, blogger and book reviewer. She is also commissioning editor for the Alliance of Independent Authors' self-publishing advice blog and a book promotion consultant.

The Department for Lessons Learned

Welcome to the District Council's Department for Lessons Learned*, the information and experience management team. We document and disseminate quarterly summaries of institutional knowledge, co-ordinate information implementation policy, and are the administrators and curators of the official Understanding Archive.

In the financial year 2023/24, we have gone a long way to joining up departments, reducing workload-duplication and encouraging inter-departmental information-sharing. However, true open information will not be achieved until the real understanding of how we work and deliver our services transcends not only individual departments, but also individual employees.

Employees are encouraged to phone the hot line or email our designated account and leave details of the information that should be known more widely within the organisation. It is stressed that failure is as valuable to the Department of Lessons Learned as success. Employees changing roles or leaving the organisation are encouraged to make at least five knowledge-collection appointments with a member of the Lessons Learned team prior to their last day.

The Department for Lessons Learned's achievements include the creation of Trusted Bin Neighbours. After a tip from a member of the public, we reduced paper usage by 63% by eliminating bin-collection calendars, informing one designated resident on each road on the day before bin collection, and providing that resident with a fluorescent bin. It has also established a Fast Failure Network, a group of council employees who critique and develop each other's policy and service re-design ideas on an ongoing basis.

. . . .

"Hi! You've reached Phoebe at the Department for Lessons Learned. I'm not currently available to speak to you, but we answer 87% of all queries by the second contact and customers report a 94% satisfaction rate with our responses, so I would recommend that you try calling back at a later time. Information indicates that I am least busy between 11 am and 12:30 pm, and least productive between 12:30 pm and 2 pm. Therefore I would recommend that you call at 12 pm. To rate your satisfaction with this message on a scale of 1 to 10, press #, then your response, then # again. Thanks!"

*A number of organisations, including the US Marine Corp. and NATO, have a department or centre for lessons learned.

. . . .

Jenny Rowlands is the Chief Executive of Lewes District Council. Her professional career combines senior management experience across housing, policy, communications, equalities and the environment. Jenny has worked on issues of diversity and inclusion throughout her career.

Phoebe Morris-Jones is the Graduate Intern at Lewes District Council. Phoebe specialises in projects at the council involving social media, digital innovation and community engagement.

Time Passing and Running

Time passing. So here I sit in 2026, staring at the past. The low points that made my bones ache were the demise of values-based, conviction politics; the media promotion of the politics of envy; the national obsession with 'what's in it for me?'

I was a council chief exec, and between 2010 and 2016 I'd laid off 2,000 staff and cut external contracts by £200 million. It was 2016-17 when the uncommitted reserves dried up and the flexible money ran out, but, mercifully, by then we had already completed a major transformation.

We'd anticipated the money running out and introduced a new approach we called 'co-operative commissioning'. Our way was about people doing more for themselves and helping others in their community to do more. We moved away from direct provision and control. We enabled and encouraged people to get involved, to step up and do.

By 2018 most authorities had either thrown in the public sector towel by completely outsourcing their services and/or shutting down activities. Not us. We held tight. Time passed.

Time running. It ain't all bad, though, and there were high points. I was the local authority representative on the bid team which won the 2026 World Cup for the UK. The tournament starts in a few months and I'm still dining out on that one. More seriously, in 2016 I was part of the National Commission that nailed the case for prevention and early intervention as the core discipline of children's services. That features high on my 'made a real difference there' list.

In my authority, our new approach created a range of social enterprises – parks, libraries and youth services – run at arms' length through local groups. All the council does now is maintain a core team of commissioning staff.

Funny thing is, that strategy, so radical in its day, became the ideological anchor for the party manifestos of all those vying for government in the 2020 UK elections. It feels like something useful came out of the period of austerity, but will it stick? Or will it disappear in time passing and running and running and passing*?

*Old Jamaican song lyric, Big Yute, Island Records 1974

. . . .

Derrick Anderson, CBE, is the Chief Executive of Lambeth Council and started in post on 1 March 2006. Derrick, who was born in London, has more than 30 years' management experience in the public sector. He is a member of the University of Birmingham Council and Social Fund Board, and is a Prince's Trust Ambassador and Vice President of UK Youth.

Ice on the Inside of the Window at No. 83

Iris' breath hung in the cold damp air and she shuddered at the thought of getting out of bed. What would Alf think of her now? Her savings all gone.

Her beloved husband, dead for ten long years. She could hear his stern but reassuring voice as she piled clothing and blankets upon her once youthful body. On his deathbed, Alf took solace in the fact that she would remain in their home and live out her life contentedly.

She remembered the first letter like it was yesterday. It said she had won £3000. All she had to do to claim it was send off £30. The odd letter turned into a drip and then a deluge. The winnings never came. Only yesterday, she had been to the Post Office and sent off another £15.

The letters looked so official, the people she spoke with on the phone so nice and friendly. She just could not comprehend. She belonged in another age. You left your doors and windows open. People cared.

The doorbell pierced the quiet. She rose from the relative warmth of the bed and struggled down the stairs.

The shadow at the door looked youthful, full of hope and energy. Iris unlocked the door carefully, making sure the chain remained on.

"Yes, who is it?"

"Trading Standards, Iris. From the Council. Let me show you my ID."

She took the card. Checked it and handed it back.

"What do you want?"

"We've been doing some work with the Post Offices round here. Mr Khan is worried you're sending off so much money. Iris, can we help? You can talk to us."

"No, thank you."

"We can help with those letters."

Again she thought of Alf, the warm house they shared, the food she used to prepare for him, watching *Strictly Come Dancing* together on TV. Deep within her soul hope stirred. She would do it for Alf.

"Come on in dear. It's a long story."

. . . .

Bob Charnley is currently Trading Standards and Licensing Manager at Sandwell Metropolitan Borough Council, with over 30 years' experience working in local government trading standards services. His specialist area of trading standards law is food standards and he is a visiting lecturer at Birmingham University.

Joined Up Now!

It's true, I admit it. I was more than miffed, way back in 2014, when all Mr Minister had to offer stressed-out council delegates at the annual public finance conference was that they could raise more cash – if electors ok'd it by referendum. But just look at us now.

It all began, of course, with the Internet of Things. You know, where everything from your fridge to your wheelie bin has a tiny computer linked to the centre, automatically telling it stuff. It was a northern district council that led the way, as it happens, joining up all their council services. Biggest impact was that it did away with a lot of call centre traffic. Public loved that. You can see that, can't you? No more uncool muzak or "Thank you for holding. Your call IS important to us." Ever.

Instead, street lights now report their own bulb failures, your wheelie bin tells the council how full it is and – this one really helped nail anti-social behavior – tenants' doors tell the noise patrol about any extended noise nuisance. Well, you get the idea. And for services without gadgets, there's a clever new mobile phone app, harnessed to Twitter of course, giving residents direct access to council services such as social care.

It wasn't all about the technology and what these gadgets actually did, though. It was more that they provoked a real tipping point in public confidence. They helped boost efficiency and effectiveness in a *transparent* way. They let the public *see* more clearly what we actually did and how we did it effectively. Public opinion was nudged, if you like. Then a virtuous spiral effect kicked in, people got talking, involved in ways they'd long forgotten. Social media helped, of course. The child saved by her wheelie bin story went viral.

So when we finally held our referendums – electronically, by mobile phone, of course – we had a resounding yes result – yes to more spending on more services. So, yes, I suppose what I really want to say is, now look at us, Mr Minister!

. . . .

Lesley Lodge is an eclectic freelance writer (housing finance, horses in film and historical crime fiction). A firm believer in the public sector, she worked previously for CIPFA (fourteen years), Southwark Council (Peckham Partnership), Sheffield City Council and HM Treasury.

Social Web, Social Value

Funnily enough, the change started from within. I can't say for sure whether it was the result of employees insisting on more fulfilling working lives or organisations tapping into workforce potential because they needed increased productivity. Perhaps it was both.

When I started out computers were like sheds, phones like bricks, we all worked in silos, even though the services were being delivered by different public and private providers. The technology quickly reinvented itself, but no-one built knowledge. It was hard to access reliable information, to find the people with the answers. I think we probably practised evidence-based policy-making without the evidence.

I began using a collaboration platform. It was designed for the public sector, but there were only small cells there at first. They were the advance guard, the evangelists. I was initially unsure of myself, but then I realised I could open a window and they could hear me and what's more they wanted to listen. I was a convert, committed to the cause.

The actual revolution came when organisations exhausted internal resource and started knocking on the doors of others. That really demolished the silos – first regionally, then nationally and ultimately globally. Data and information, expertise and knowledge, original and authentic, traded openly and securely.

The results were incredible. I suddenly leapt from my small pod to being part of a global movement. Not only was I empowered, but I also realised that no one person holds all the truth.

We called it a social intranet. To me it just built bridges between people and conversations. Working together was a given and everyone could draw on these connections, wherever, however and whenever they wanted. Not only could I trust what I found, I now had a voice and finally it had impact.

. . . .

Jason Fahy is Executive Director of Knowledge Hub (www.khub. net), a free-to use-digital collaboration platform dedicated to creating social value.

Open Doors

Aislin descended the cellar steps for the third time that week, her first in local government, looking for archived invoices. It was summer 1984 and her boss had just been telling her about the Local Government Act 1972 and some funny anecdotes related to the reorganisation of 1974. From the little she could glean, not much had changed in the last ten years.

She was prone to spooky experiences and, as cool air brushed her cheek, she hoped this was not one of those occasions. Instead of boxes, at the bottom of the steps there were three doors, each with a sign.

The first, on a polished brass plate, said 'Local Government 1984'; the second, on a brushed metal sign, said 'Local Government 2014'; and the third, handmade, read 'Local Choice 2024'. Curiosity took over. After all, doors are meant to be opened.

She opened the first door. Through a misty haze, she saw herself a few months later, bounding up the steps of her local college. She was somewhat surprised at her enthusiasm.

Behind the second, she saw herself presenting at an important meeting. While she was lost in thought about how she looked, the image moved on to the strange form of presentation and she noticed her title, 'Chief Executive', and the heading, 'Options for Future Models of Local Government'.

Still shocked, she shakily opened the third door. She saw herself, age 59, and felt dizzy. As she regained composure, she could see the delight on her future face as she made an announcement to a virtual audience.

"I am honoured to accept the role of Prime Resident of Eireton. Heading up this new PC* enterprise is an exciting challenge, ten years in the making. I would like to thank the local votership. A turnout of 90% via our local choice portal is remarkable. I look forward to working closely with the City Partnership and its newly elected executive."

Aislin wondered why her future had been revealed by such an unusual experience. Still shaking, she thought, "Am I really destined to make a difference...? Now, where's that invoice."

*Publicly controlled

. . . .

Lisa Quinn has 27 years' experience in local government and was Director of Finance and Business Services at Cheshire East Council before joining Capita Asset Services in June 2013. Prior to this role, Lisa was Corporate Manager, Finance & Assets at Macclesfield Borough Council, where she worked for 22 years.

Subject K Finds a New Role

K is a complex character. We have worked together over several sessions and it has become clear that the subject combines four different personalities. However, at no point do these other personalities take over. You wouldn't know they were there, but they are shaping and reshaping, silently constructing from within.

I take K's words and deeds, forensically peeling back thought-processes; dissecting different influences; seeing what might be attributable to distinct beings.

The oldest one, Joe, is staid, strict, with immense reserves of energy, ambition and pride. He points to dynasties from which he inherited obligations and moral standards that no-one can ever live up to. Joe sits in stern judgement.

The youngest, Sue, feels at risk, to the point of paranoia. She is worried and uncertain, with occasional acts of self-harm. She deals with life through endless checklists and Post-it plans. She spent in the past, but now faces an empty purse.

The other two are male, making Sue feel even more vulnerable. Harold, the older one, is Welsh, non-conformist, "rough-handed, but smooth-talking". He claims to be ex-army and a former civil servant in India. He reflects a need for structures, commands, controls; the very stuff of Empire.

Alan is an engineer, full of visions, missions and management-speak. Where Joe and Harold are dedicated to creating, Alan is intent on running things; extending the reach; pushing the boundaries; making the difference.

Every day K wrestles with these varying demands, without even recognising they are there. Today's breakthrough was the realisation of a way forward. If K could only find a role that picked out the best of everyone then that would free up the spirit, refresh the sense of purpose. The right role would give Joe no grounds for moral objection, would satisfy Harold's need for duty, would still allow Alan to make the difference, and would free Sue from anxiety.

. . . .

Geoff Bateson is an independent writer and researcher, based in Birmingham. He has had a career of more than 40 years in a local authority context. Geoff has published four ebooks and spoken at a wide range of national and international conferences. His work can be found at www.thewordsthething.org.uk

It Pays to Care

"Open to all, coerced by none!" That was the motto of the local paper and Jon was its newest reporter. As he headed off for his first assignment, he figured his granddad, Harry, would've been proud.

As soon as he walked into Spring House, Jon was reminded of the place where he used to visit Harry, up north, while he was still alive. The big lounge, loud television and well-worn chairs were all familiar. The memories were mixed, though. Harry started to get confused easily there and, by the end, he didn't really remember who Jon was. Still, that was a long time ago now and Jon had an interview to do.

"This is a *care home*," said Grace, without needing much prompting. "Me and all the other ladies work here because we want people to feel cared for, in a place that feels like home. I think it's one of the most important things we can do as a society. We don't do it for the money, really.

"It is hard, though, when you put in every shift you can and still you can't afford a Christmas present for your son. I can't remember the last time our family went on holiday. But last month all of us here got a pay rise – a living wage, the council calls it. It's made a difference. I can afford to catch the tube to work now, instead of two buses, which means I can get a bit more sleep in the morning and a little more time with my boy, Dean, when I get home."

At the end of their interview, Jon put his cup down in its saucer, thanked Grace and was about to leave when Arthur, in the next chair, grabbed his hand the way Harry used to whenever he had something important to say. "We're not always easy to look after, us lot," he said, with a grin. "But they do a grand job. It's a hard day's work. They should get paid enough to live on."

. . . .

Councillor **Andy Hull** is an elected member for Highbury West and the Executive Member for Finance and Performance at the London Borough of Islington. He co-chaired the Islington Fairness Commission and is a leading activist on the national Sharkstoppers and Living Wage campaigns.

To Hell in a Handcart

His aunty's flat is hot and loud. They're celebrating Samuel's last night in Lagos, drinking like kings, enjoying genuine label Hennessy's washed down with the bitter malt of Guinness. They're eating like chiefs. The peppery ears of a goat's head peek out of a lake of oily stew.

"Ah! Even Usain Bolt can't keep up with the Nigerian economy. You should move back-O!" A cousin slaps his shoulder. "Hi-tech start-up? Why not?" An Arsenal match is on TV. The screen's almost as big as the one in his lounge back in Dagenham. On a night like this, Sam could be tempted.

Instead he avoids the question, stumbling slightly out onto the balcony. The sulphurous smell of rubbish nearly knocks him over. A sign on the fortress compound opposite warns "Beware of 419. This house is not for sale." Hundreds of people walk by in the pavement-less, potholed road, selling what they can. Aunty Asi demands money for his niece's school fees. Even if he was a security guard in London, he couldn't refuse. They think he's a big man, a hot-shot IT manager.

Sam knows he's really good at his job, but he hasn't told them he works for the local council. They would laugh. They would howl like a pack of wild dogs. They'd assume he was on the take. Although he's proud of his heritage, this place does his head in. It's unreal. His father always talked about the old days, the British system of local government they'd inherited, but he's glad his old man isn't around to see the hollow shell Lagos has become.

Man, he's drunker than he thought. Even the shell has been shattered and no one's gluing it together. Suddenly morose, he thinks maybe this is the future for Dagenham. Is this where we're heading? He sends his niece to get him a cold Coke and tries to break his downward spiral. OK, his borough could be better, but the system works. In fact, he knows it can be better and he'll say his piece, do what he can to hold it together. East London's his home and he's staying put.

. . . .

Uchenna Dickson Ogbonna describes himself as a persistently positive public servant. He has lived and worked in Nigeria and the UK. This story is the result of a collaboration with Dawn Reeves.

Taking a Lead

William Jackson stood up from his desk, pulled on his tweed jacket and strode out of his office. This daily ritual, a walk through the city at lunchtime, was usually just about enjoying the fresh air, but today he found himself in a more reflective mood.

Walking down the high street and onto the waterfront, he considered the time he had spent working in this city. His intention had been to stay for a couple of years and then move somewhere bigger, more exciting – this city had seemed such a sleepy place. But something had got under his skin and somehow two years turned into five, and then ten, and now he realised it was three decades and he was the senior partner.

As he strolled along the waterfront, with the lively bars and restaurants full of people enjoying the late summer sunshine, he remembered the meeting at the council offices all those years ago. Back then, he saw the council as the body that sent your rates bill. Back then, concepts like 'place-shaping' and 'city-centre renewal strategies' were not something a local lawyer thought about, never mind actually got involved in!

He'd gone along to that meeting expecting the usual political plati-tudes about why the council couldn't do this or that, why the new road scheme, long-promised but never delivered, was going to be delayed yet again.

Until that moment he'd never really considered how places came about – they were just there. And even if he had thought about it, well, what would politicians and local bureaucrats know about creating growth?

To his surprise, what he had found were people passionate about the place, who genuinely wanted to work with local businesses like his, to make this city, *his* city, better. And it had inspired him, revealed a passion that still inspired him on his daily walk.

What he found was leadership. And it had dawned on him that actually that's what brings about change – leadership. It was leadership that created vision; leadership that had awoken his sleepy city, and him, for the future.

. . . .

John Latham is currently a director at the City of Lincoln Council, having worked in corporate management, neighbourhood renewal and regeneration for the last 25 years. Outside of work John is mostly a taxi driver for his 12-year-old daughter, filling his time in between by supporting Leeds United.

Welcome to Peoplestown

Following the council elections in Peoplestown, there was a change of administration and a new council leader was appointed. This new leader was determined to make a difference for local people and their place.

The council was well regarded, its services either good or better. Its senior management team were good, but focused on their services and the council, as the previous political administration had been.

The new leader and her group wanted to improve service quality, but they wanted to do more. They recognised that something was missing. And so did local people.

The leader had long supported local community activism, like many of her group colleagues. She was energetic, values-driven and passionate for her community, for the people and for working across Peoplestown.

The new leader recognised that, on its own, the council could not address the local social, economic and environmental challenges, and it would have to work evermore closely with the NHS, the police, other public agencies, the voluntary and community sector, and local businesses. Above all, the council would need a new relationship with local people. It would need to communicate, engage with, listen to and involve them – all of them.

The leader decided to drive her and her group's vision for Peoplestown by creating a cabinet that reflected the community, in terms of the people appointed and their portfolios. There would be no portfolio directly related to a council department or directorate, and all cabinet members would have cross-cutting responsibilities for partnership working, collaboration, community empowerment, citizen engagement, growth and development. There was a collective will based on shared values and policies. Orthodoxy would always be challenged.

Cabinet members would work with civil society, the voluntary and community sector, local businesses and the wider public sector. There would be joint executive and non-executive boards involving these partners, too. And cabinet members, both collectively and individually, would talk with and involve citizens. Money would be allocated to support and grow community and voluntary sector capacity.

The Leader often repeated the mantra, "It's all about Peoplestown and its people, not the council." After a few years the results were clear for all to see and feel.

. . . .

John Tizard is a strategic advisor and commentator on public policy and public services. His approach is 'collaborating and challenging for excellence'.

Three Breaks and a Retirement

The Granny Smith swung late in the overcast conditions of the budgetary control section of the London Borough of Thames.

It was March, the budget was set, the cricket season loomed, any opportunity for a practice was to be seized. Fast bowler Joel launched the Granny Smith as usual. Brian flung out a hand desperately, but the apple eluded him. It crashed through the third floor window and shattered on the bonnet of the chief solicitor's new car. Fortunately this was one breakage that was quickly repaired.

Brian was looking back after 41 years in local government. About to retire, it was time to reflect. He had gone through cuts, booms, CCT*, best value, more cuts and now austerity.

He also reflected on a running career that had peaked in the nineties with a two hour 30-minute London Marathon, followed by the Maidstone County Championships. In fourth position at 21 miles with the leaders in sight, Brian had felt a bump from behind and found himself lying in the road, his leg bent at a ridiculous angle. He'd realised his race was over. That break meant four weeks in hospital.

The noughties found him leading a local government bête noir, the 'private finance initiative', otherwise known as PFI. Standing in a classroom at the borough's largest school, Brian watched a young teacher attempt to impart the finer points of English grammar while a Siberian blast hurtled through a broken window. These breakages had not received such urgent treatment.

However, the much-criticised PFI righted a wrong and delivered a new school fit for the 21st century and, as retirement beckoned, Brian felt he had helped to change the ending for at least the next few generations of pupils who would pass through the new school.

He recalled his favourite phrase: "We are still on the planet." Yes, whatever the attacks on local government, people would still need their refuse collected, their loved ones buried, their old folk looked after and somewhere for their kids to play. Local government would always have a part to play in changing these endings for the better.

*Compulsory competitive tendering

. . . .

Mike Ellsmore has recently retired as Director of Finance and Resources at the London Borough of Bexley. He is a CIPFA member and was involved at regional level. He is a keen runner with a marathon personal best of 2 hours 30 minutes – although some years ago!

I Know that Goat

Barry? You must remember Barry – Finance Officer – ended up in Parking Control; shortish; comb-over; trousers always looked a size-and-a-half too big.

Got his first job aged 14, just out of school: filling municipal coals-cuttles. Imagine a grubby-kneed boy, socks round ankles lugging a brass bucket up to the Mayor's Parlour. They'd a grate in every room of the Town Hall in those days.

That was in the 1940s. Hitler still dropping free samples on Hackney, Dad in the army, Mum out charring, plenty of mouths to feed, Barry doing his bit.

At 16 he got a promotion – collecting pennies from the slots in the Ladies and Gents. Plenty of public lavs in those days. Did you know George Bernard Shaw stood for Camden Council on that very issue? – a mark of civilisation *he* said. Barry'd empty the leather collecting-bag onto the desk, pile up those big brown coins: King one side, Britannia the other: 12 pennies to a shilling, 20 shillings in a pound.

Married? Oh yes, 50 years or more. He knew Dora from when they were kids: a clever girl: rose to be a top secretary. See, in those days councils trained the talented. Sometimes one of the bosses'd dictate an urgent report over the blower; she'd be on headphones, fingers flying. Perfect copy every time. There's no automatic correction facility in a typewriter!

Only one kid – lovely girl, Theresa. Wouldn't go to university; only cared about animals; became an Animal Warden. Funny isn't it? In councils we look after everyone: pensioners, kids, animals…

The other day I'm driving down Viccy Park Road; suddenly this goat comes galloping towards me – middle of the road *against the one-way system* – a blooming great Billy, with curly horns.

Back at the office I call Theresa.

"I know that goat!" she says. "Leave it to me."

You know what, I felt a bit sorry for old Billy – he'd be no match for Theresa.

Yes, his death was a shock. Didn't seem fair somehow, so soon after retirement. Big turnout. Not bad for someone in Parking Control.

. . . .

Stephanie Brann worked in the charitable sector and for several London local authorities. Once her specialisms included older and disabled people, the crossovers between housing and social care, benefits, adaptations and disrepair. Now she's writing a novel. She remains admiring of the front-line workers who carry on the good work.

The Interview

"Can I get you a drink?"

"No, this water is fine... Thank you."

"OK, I'll let the panel know you've arrived."

Not sure I can bear this... The waiting... thinking... sweating.

Right, pull yourself together. Focus. What did they say on the website? What are they looking for?

Demonstrate your 'communication skills'. Written, fine, but I did struggle with presentations at school. How embarrassing! I wasn't up for standing at the front, all the attention on me, trying to find the right words and not sound too different from the other kids. But my confidence grew, my English got better and while they might pick up a twang, I reckon I'm pretty confident in front of a crowd now.

But how do I show 'enthusiasm for the subject'? Well, this gets to the heart of it. Politics is what got me here. Rooms full of blokes banging on about their philosophy, their ideolology, while the bombs dropped outside never got my people anywhere. I want to break that cycle.

It also said to show I've worked 'independently'. That made me chuckle. How about travelling across Europe in the back of a lorry? Now that's independent travel! Still, I can't say I was on my own once I'd met Cate. If it wasn't for my social worker I'd probably still be camped in France, trying to jump on the next lorry. She was awesome, the first warm, friendly person I'd seen for months.

I remember Gaza felt so far away when I arrived, cold, wet and on my own. Not a great start for a 13-year-old, but I was lucky. They might have been strangers, but they were there for me, supported me, trusted me. These people took me in and wanted nothing in return. A home, education, even a job this summer. I worked in IT. How funny – me in the IT crowd! I owe them stacks.

The heavy oak door swings open.

"Jalal, can you come through now please?"

Deep breath. Let's go make those guys proud.

. . . .

Graeme McDonald spent 15 years working in local government and is currently Director of SOLACE.

About Shared Press

SHARED PRESS

Shared Press is an independent publisher with a remit to share stories that engage with the sharp edges and messy boundaries of modern life; to give voice to new writers who care about ideas and innovation; and to inspire new creative conversations with readers. **Additional stories from the Change the Ending project will be published on the Shared Press website in 2014 – see sharedpress.co.uk**

More from Shared Press
It's a small list, but it's perfectly formed and it's growing

HARD CHANGE

Published by Shared Press in 2012, Dawn Reeves' *Hard Change* is set in and around the local council of a medium-sized Midlands city and centres on the compelling ramifications of the murder of a young girl. Neither a traditional political thriller nor a conventional crime novel, it focuses on strategy rather than procedure and examines whether – and how – individual and collective action can make a difference.

WE KNOW WHAT WE ARE

Dawn Reeves' sequel to Hard Change, *We Know What We Are*, will be published by Shared Press in 2015. In a city on the brink of bankruptcy, the first Asian woman to lead the council, a teenage girl in care and an accountant in denial about his gambling addiction form an unlikely alliance to solve a murder, take on the might of the local football club and grapple with identity, choice and power. **For updates on new projects and titles, see sharedpress.co.uk**

Lightning Source UK Ltd.
Milton Keynes UK
UKOW03f1145111014

239938UK00002B/7/P